Marco

Brian Leon Lee

Brian. Leon Lee

ISBN-10: 1079730443
ISBN-13: 9781079730449

The Author

The author was born in Manchester. On leaving school, a period in accountancy was followed by a teaching career in Primary Education.

He is the writer of several children's short stories including the popular Bouncey the Elf.

A keen Sci-fi reader for more years than he would like to remember, Trimefirst was his first endeavour in this genre, followed by Domain of the Netherworld and Spectre of El Dorado.

Now retired and living in South Yorkshire.

By Brian Leo Lee
(Children's stories)
Bouncey the Elf and Friends Bedtime Stories
Just Bouncey
Bouncey the Elf and Friends Meet Again
Bouncey the Elf and Friends (Box Set)

Four Tales from Sty-Pen

Mr Tripsy's Trip
Mr Tripsy's Boat Trip

By Brian Leon Lee
Trimefirst
Domain of the Netherworld
The Club
Spectre of El Dorado

All available as eBooks

http://www.bounceytheelf.co.uk

For

Rita

1

'Wow, what a f.... fantastic view,' Chaz Lorimore said, as he leaned closer to the apartment window and looked down forty-seven storeys to watch the scurrying, ant-like people, dash across a road junction before the lights changed.

He looked further down the road and saw serried ranks of similar high-rise apartment blocks as far as the eye could see.

Turning back into the room, he looked over to Esha Leung, a dark haired veterinary assistant in a State Park of Queensland, Australia and coughed into his hand.

'Err, it's a bit different from the Andes.'

'Esha gave a laugh and looked over at her Uncle Jinhai sitting opposite her at the dining table.

'Just look at him Uncle. He's actually blushing.'

'Now now, Esha, stop being a tease. From what you have told me, Chaz has never been to Hong Kong before.'

Jinhai Chen, a recently retired professor of chemistry, was quite tall and still had a good head of silvery hair and a wispy moustache which now twitched, as he pointed to the dining chair opposite him and said, 'Take no notice of her Chaz. She is just behaving like that cheeky monkey I knew. What was it, Esha, ten - twelve years ago when you....'

'Don't you dare tell Chaz that story, he'll think I'm a moron or something worse.'

Chaz sniggered and got an elbow in his ribs as he sat down next to her.

'Now that you two have calmed down, try some of

my herbal tea. Made from of seven different herbs, no less plus my, what you say, magic ingredient.' And he poured from an ancient looking porcelain teapot a golden stream of amber coloured liquid into their cut glass tumblers.

'While you are enjoying that, I'll go and get that bit of family history that we talked about, Esha. Okay.'

After a perfunctory sniff, Chaz took a sip and then another and then licked his lips.

"Bloody hell, it's got a kick like a mule. What did you say your Uncle was, Esha?'

'A chemist, he was a Professor of Chemistry.'

*Chaz and Esha had met up in Bolivia earlier that year. An unusual event had catapulted them, along with two other new friends, into a lethal, bitter conflict with, of all things, the Conquistadors of South America. ***

Nobody believed them of course. So after a week or two of coming back to reality, Esha suggested to Chaz, that maybe he would like to meet up with her in Hong Kong.

Her Uncle, she explained, had mentioned a few times that her family ancestry had connections with Dunhuang, a town on the Old Silk Road.

Chaz was intrigued enough to say that he still had a few weeks left of his end of Uni holiday and agreed to meet her in Kowloon.

Uncle Jinhai returned carrying an old, scruffy cardboard file and sat down opposite them, saying as he opened it, 'Most of what I have in here is not of much interest to you, Esha but when I came across a mention of a certain Jinhai Chen, my namesake would you believe, during the time of Marco Polo and that he was reported to have helped save his life, this is what I found.'

* Spectre of El Dorado

—

2

'Wow,' Chaz pricked up his ears. At least he had heard of Marco Polo – who hadn't.'

'Have a look,' and her Uncle passed a tattered piece of discoloured parchment to her.

Esha took hold of the document, looked at it for a few seconds and then she suddenly cried out.

'I don't believe it. The writing, it's in old Mandarin script.'

As far as Chaz was concerned, it could have been in Double Dutch.

'So,' he said, 'What's special about that?'

'Well,' Esha leaned forward in excitement.

'To be able to write in Mandarin in the thirteenth century you had to come from the richer class or be a trained government official.'

She looked over to her Uncle and pressed his arm.

'Oooh, do you think this Jinhai Chen could have been in charge of the Dunhuang caravanserai?'

'Maybe. What a nice idea but that is something that we shall never know, Esha.'

'Well, I want to go to Dunhuang, now more than ever. We might find out something more about this saving of Marco Polo. What do say Chaz?'

Chaz looked at Esha. He'd come this far, so what the hell.

'I'm in,' he said.

'Oh, I'm so glad,' she said, as she buried him in a pleasantly tight cuddle.

Uncle Jinhai smiled at them and then said, 'If that's the case, I have something that might be very useful. The Gobi desert is full of all sorts of creepy crawlies.'

He stood and went over to a corner unit and rummaged in it for a minute before picking up a slim narrow plastic box.

'It contains six sealed patches of antitoxin inhibitors that I developed before I retired. Unfortunately, lab politics got in the way of its commercial development. One of the reasons I retired,' he said ruefully, as he handed the box to Esha.

Being a veterinary assistant, Esha was well aware of the danger of catching nasty bugs and things and she stood and gave her Uncle a hug of thanks.

Shortly after they had said bye to her Uncle, Esha and Chaz were making their way down one of Hong Kong's giant escalators in order to catch a MTR (Mass Transit Railway) connection to their overnight hostel.

On the way down, Esha used her smart phone to book their rail tickets to Dunhuang via Lanzhou, a journey of around twenty-six hours.

As usual, Esha was chattering ten to the dozen and Chaz, not a great traveller at the best of times, gamely tried to keep his eyes open as well as avoiding bumping into what must be half of the world's population.

2

Chaz clung to the handrail of the carriage and eased himself down onto the station platform.

Dunhuang. They had actually made it. Jeez, what a journey. The least said about it the better, he thought. *Battery hens had more bloody space then this chuffin' train (No pun intended). The 'rail hard-sleeper' carriages — Who was the cretin that gave it that name — he was bleeding right about that though, had two lots of three narrow, wafer thin bunk-beds set in alcoves all along one side of the carriage. Each with a curtain for privacy.*

Of course, brainbox had forgot that people bring luggage with them. So the passage was chock-a-block with stuff. It took a good twenty minutes of pushing, twisting and climbing to get to that crappy buffet-bar or toilet.

Jeez, the first soddin' time we went, they found out that you had to bring your own cup for any sort of drink, for God's sake. Sods law that he lost the toss of the coin and had to go back for the plastic cups they fortunately had in their daypacks left on their beds.

Fortunately, they had been given the two top ones. A great advantage Chaz found was that his feet were able to stretch out over the corridor, way above anyone passing along it. A boon for the taller guy.

The occupants of the beds below had no extra room like that, as the alcove wall was in the way.

He thanked the Gods who had also arranged the four elderly Buddhists, on a holy visit to the Mogao Caves, near Dunhuang, to this alcove. They made great guards when he and Esha were both away. They had become her slaves when she gave each one a packet of rice cakes.

Four or was it five more time they had to do that soddin' trip,

5

nature waits for no one of course............

'Chaz, Chaz, are you okay, you look terrible.' Esha grasped hold of Chaz by his arm tightly and he looked groggily at her.

'Uh. Oh, sorry. I think this trip is one step too far and he gave a great big yawn, followed by what he thought was a great big grin.'

'Don't look at me like that,' she snapped back.

'I'm just as tired as you. So just watch it okay.'

'Hey, hey, I didn't mean anything.'

They had both stopped in the middle of the crowded platform, blocking the way for several groups of travellers who had to part quickly in order to go around them. Many gave a disapproving glance at what they thought was unseemly behavior in public.

They stared at each other for a few moments and Chaz saw a twitch in one of Esha's eyes and he started to smile and she in turn broke into a grin and it was over.

The taxi only took five minutes to reach the grandly named Dunhuang Silk Road Hostel. A further ten minutes later they were shown to their basic uni-like bedrooms, men to the left, women to the right.

Since they had arrived in Dunhuang just after eight am in the morning, they had agreed to catch-up on the lost sleep and then meet hopefully around 13hrs for a meal in the hostel buffet bar.

Of course Chaz needed a knock or two before he called out that he'd be down soon.

They were both naturally refreshed after their sleep and ready for their first proper meal for over twenty odd hours.

He gave Esha a wave when he saw her by a window table and sat down.

'I recommend the yellow noodles with meat and vegetables but try this first, Chaz.'

Chaz picked up a chilled glass of a pale yellow liquid and tasted it. 'Not bad, not bad at all. What is it? I seem to recall the taste but I'm not sure now.'

Esha smiled. 'Well it's actually rather special and was first made in Dunhuang.'

She laughed as she said, 'Now don't throw up. It's made by boiling apricot peel and of course some other secret ingredients.'

Chaz nodded and took another drink. 'As I said, not too bad. Not bad at all.'

3

They left the hostel shortly after finishing their meal, feeling quite human again for the first time in ages.

It was hot, 30c plus and Esha was wearing a straw dŏuli (conical) hat.

Chaz need no urging. As a redhead he knew the necessity of protecting himself in hot sunny conditions and his khaki jungle hat's wide brim did the trick.

Their sunglasses were also essential in cutting down the glare.

The weight of his daypack pulled at his shoulders and he eased one of the straps.

Esha had persuaded him to bring it, saying that in Bolivia she had learnt never to take anything for granted. You never know what you might need, was her motto from now on.

For once he didn't argue and had brought his along.

The clatter of an approaching engine made Chaz look down the road.

A shabby looking single decker bus had arrived, its windows scratched and etched by years of sand particles being blown by strong winds and blasted against them.

The destination plate, next to the driver, could just be deciphered through the mucky windscreen. It read in Mandarin – Crescent Moon Lake.

'Ooh aren't we lucky,' Esha said. 'That's one of the places I was telling you about, Chaz. Come on, there's a crowd already at the shuttle bus stop.'

They hurried the last fifty or so metres and Esha said, 'Even you Chaz, can't get lost on this bus trip. It only goes there and back.'

Chaz pretended to ignore that remark. He was more concerned by the pushy bastard behind him, who kept crowding his space. Then the cheeky bugger, would you believe, suddenly gobbed to the ground just missing his foot.

'What the hell.'

'Shush Chaz, you'll cause a scene,' whispered Esha.

'Me. Me, cause a scene. He nearly spat on my boot.'

'You're in China. They do things different here.'

'So I bloody well see.'

'Please Chaz keep it quiet. The bus driver is looking at you. He won't let you on if you keep making a fuss.'

Jeez, it seems as though a terrorist would get more respect round here than me, thought Chaz but he held his tongue –just and they found their seats.

It was stifling inside the shuttle despite each side window's slider being open and damned uncomfortable, thought Chaz, as sweat dripped down his face. *No chuffin' air-conditioning either. Typical, what a place.*

He fiddled with his daypack perched on his knee and prayed that the M15 goon driver up front would get going.

Esha unzipped a side pocket of her daypack and produced two hand held battery operated fans.

'Here Chaz, this should help,' she said, passing him one with a satisfied – I told you so – look on her face.

With as much grace as he could muster, Chaz took it and turned it on.

A gentle but cool breeze wafted his face and he laughed and gave her the thumbs up, feeling much better already.

Then the shuttle bus engine rattled into life and five minutes later they were trundling along a wide, arrow straight tree – lined boulevard towards the highest sand dunes Chaz had ever seen. They were at least one hundred metres high.

The shuttle stopped some way short of them and Esha, having replaced the fans, said, 'It looks as if there is a barrier of sorts across the road.'

They let the rush of eager sightseers get off first and left the shuttle bus, just stopping to put their daypacks on.

Along the left side of the road, a line of vendor stalls and tents were trying to cater for the whims of the tourist, displaying a huge variety of bright and gaudy handicrafts.

Walking slowly, not only because of the heat, Chaz, casually eyed what was on offer. Of course the main theme was the Crescent Moon Lake. It was remarkable how much ingenuity had been used to incorporate the one idea. Then he paused.

'Hang on, hang on a moment, Esha.'

A scruffy, Bedouin type tent had caught his attention.

In fact, it wasn't the tent as such, more the figure squatting in the shade of the awning.

He wore a brightly patterned silk robe, with a red sash round his waist. A black, shallow flower-pot style hat covered the few lanks of silvery hair struggling to reach his shoulders. His hands, placed on his knees were hidden inside the wide sleeves of the robe.

A wispy goatee beard couldn't hide the million wrinkles that lined his face.

Something pulled him like a magnet towards the figure and the drone of a chant emanating quietly from the old man stopped as he looked up and saw Chaz.

It was the eyes. They were golden amber in colour,

so strange and hypnotic and the sudden glance from the old man made Chaz shudder and stop.

'Hang on, hang on for a moment Esha,' he heard himself say.

Next to the squatting figure was a small brass table on top of which lay an ornate brass tray complete with a set of tiny tea bowls. Along with them was a small gaz stove gently heating a beautifully gilded kettle, from which came a plume of steam.

'I say Chaz, why have you stopped?' asked Esha, in a slightly annoyed voice as she walked back up to him.

'Fancy some tea.'

As it happened, Esha had a sudden thought that a bowl of Chinese tea was a great idea.

'I.....' She stopped for a moment, unsure again, then a feeling of warmth and well-being rushed through her.

'What a good idea, Chaz, I guess we go inside. I can't see any chairs out here.'

She looked at the shabby tent and whispered, 'I hope it's cleaner inside.'

The old man pointed to the entrance of the tent and carefully picked up and carried the tray of tea things and followed them in. As he put the tray down on a larger brass table he gave a toothed gap smile and said in Mandarin, 'I Sulu, welcome you to my humble abode. May your ancestors rest in peace.'

'Oooh, did you hear that Chaz. Oh, sorry, he has just made us welcome.'

'I bet,' he whispered, 'That's what he tells all of his customers. Just wait until he gives you the bill.'

'Quiet, he'll hear you.'

Esha was pleasantly surprised. The inside, carpeted though sparsely furnished, was as clean as one could expect, being right next to several huge sand dunes.

To the left as they entered were several cloth-covered stools, so they quietly chose a couple and sat down.

The old man fussed with the tea things after he had taken a small black cube of wood from a nearby chest.

'What the hell,' whispered Chaz as he saw the old man take a wicked looking knife from inside his robe and start to shave a few slivers of wood into the tea bowls.

'I'm not drinking that chuffin' brew, no way.' Chaz was gob smacked at what he was seeing.

'Oh my God,' Esha whispered back.'

'Don't you see, he's not Chinese. He's a Tibetan. That's not wood; it's a compressed tea block. It was so precious in Tibet that it actually became a currency.'

Chaz wasn't convinced but when the boiling water was infused with the – whatever – a sweet smell rose up from the black liquid – tea. It was tea and then he noticed a tiny dab of butter practically all melted floating on the top.

'Ugh.'

'Chaz,' whispered Esha, 'Close your eyes. It tastes better that way at first.'

He carefully took a sip.

Well, he was still on the face of the earth and he took another that emptied the bowl.

He actually attempted a smile of thanks to the old man who, would you believe, winked at him before clapping his hands.

Esha joined in. 'Well done Chaz. At least you didn't throw up like I did the first time I drank Tibetan tea.'

Feeling like he had just won a race, Chaz looked around the tent more carefully as Esha and the old man gabbed away in Mandarin.

He noticed a sort of alcove in the corner covered with a curtain. He was sure that he had just seen a flicker of violet light behind it. So getting up from his stool he slowly edged his way over and took a peek. The others never noticed. They were still talking ten to the dozen.

He nearly collapsed in shock. A brushed steel-frame with a translucent screen of about two metres by two meters square, was pulsating with a regular beat.

He went closer and saw along the bottom bar, some scuffed letters and numbers, ...eck- 24. . 9

'Naw,' he said to himself. 'It's impossible. A teleport portal here in 2019, I'm chuffin' dreaming. I know it's that soddin' tea. I bet the old devil drugged us. Just wait till I tell Esha. She fell for it hook line and sinker.'

Just then he heard an explosion. It sounded as though it was coming from the Crescent Moon Lake area and he ducked out of the alcove.

'Chaz, Chaz.' Esha was standing facing the tent entrance shaking like a leaf, broken tea bowls and a steaming kettle by her feet.

'What's happening? What shall we do?'

4

Before he could speak the old man shouted out in Mandarin, 'You must leave. They may come here. Go.' And he pointed to the portal.

'It must be a terrorist attack,' Chaz called out to Esha. He had guessed what the old man had said and he rushed over to the stools and grabbed their daypacks.

'For God's sake move it Esha.' The urgency in his voice broke the spell that had transfixed her to the floor, unable to move.

'W.... where to?'

'Never mind, just follow me,' and Chaz turned round and ran awkwardly, carrying their packs into the alcove with Esha two steps behind.

As they ran towards the pulsating screen, the old man screamed something out in Mandarin but Chaz fearing the worse, grabbed Esha by the hand and jumped through the pulsating portal, dragging a screaming Esha along with him.

The sandy ground was hard and Chaz was only able to keep on his feet because of Esha clinging like a limpet to his arm.

The smell of a decaying half-decomposed lizard swarming with ants and clouds of flies, jerked Chaz back to his senses. They had landed in some sort of rubbish heap, which appeared to be part of an old pit of some kind. A trench, lined with cut stone, headed up the slope of a sand dune from what appeared to be a stagnant pond. The scum had more or less dried out in the oppressive heat from the look of the hard crust of its surface.

'Ugh. Get us out of here, Chaz. It stinks like hell.'

'You don't have to tell me. I think the only way out is up so let's go.'

Then he had a thought.

'Just a minute, we need to know where we are.'

He turned round and was only just able to make out the pulsating portal in the brilliant sunlight, which was hidden behind a large gnarled saxaul tree. It was a wonder that it hadn't skewered them when they jumped through the portal.

'By the way Esha, what was the old man shouting when we left in such a hurry?'

'Well, it sounded like, be back before sunset.'

Chaz nodded as he handed her pack to her and thought the easiest way was to follow the trench up the slope of the sand dune.

'You know what Chaz,' Esha said, pausing for a breath. The dune was steeper than she thought.

'What.'

'That smell, it seems to be following us.'

'Don't be daft, how can a smell follow you? Come on, I want to see what's on the other side of this dune.'

A few more minutes of panting up the slope it flattened out and they saw it.

'Look at that Chaz,' Esha pointed ahead to a squat building lying a hundred or so metres away to their right.

The trench went straight towards it and as they hurried to the building the sound of running water came from it, followed by a monstrous stench.

'Oh my God,' cried Esha in disgust. 'That trench is the sewer of the caravanserai. I remember now. The camels are put in stalls along one side and their urine

15

and stuff drops down into a sloping sewer and is carried away from the caravanserai site.'

'Jeez, do you mean to tell me that we have been walking by a stinking sewer for all this time. Hang on; I nearly dived into that chuffin' pond down there. Ugh, I feel sick.'

5

A line of camels was just entering the arched main gate, designed to be wide and high enough to accommodate a fully laden beast.

Esha was trying to remember what else she knew about a caravanserai and said,

The main thing is the square, open to the sky courtyard. You need space to unload the goods and then to get the animals out of the hot sun, so the animal stalls go all round the inner wall. Remember Chaz, donkeys and horses are used as well to carry stuff. A well is usually in the centre of the courtyard, which makes sense when all the animals are all round the walls.

The merchants and their servants and guards, will probably have small rooms or niches above the animals. The Caravanserai owner will provide fodder for a fee of course...'

She was suddenly interrupted by Chaz who shouted out.

'What the hell. Just look at that. Am I dreaming or what?'

He was pointing at a patch of green next to a crescent-moon shaped lake shimmering in the sunlight.

Esha looked past the end of the Caravanserai and down towards a dip between the next huge sand dune.

Unbelievably, a lake had formed there. It was the shape that had caused Chaz to call out.

'It's got to be the same one as the one we know near Dunhuang but how....' he trailed off.

'The portal Chaz. It's got to be the portal. It actually worked.'

They looked down at the beautiful sight. No wonder so many paintings were made and photos taken. It was breathtaking.

'Yeah, we now know where we are but *when* are we?'

Esha was half petrified and exhilarated at the same time.

'Even if we know *when* we are, I don't want to spend the rest of my life here. Do you?'

Chaz kicked a small rock. 'Well, why don't we go and talk to someone in the Holiday Inn,' he said pointing to the Caravanserai.

'Don't get funny on me now Chaz, this is serious.' Esha bit her lower lip. 'Well at least you made a good suggestion, let's go and see what's happening.'

A rough looking guard holding the biggest sword Chaz had ever seen stopped them at the gate.

'Where are your camels?' he asked in old Mandarin.

Thinking fast, Esha turned and pointed to the lake. 'Down there with our family.'

The guard shrugged and moved aside and let them enter. He didn't even bother about their garb. *Travellers wore the most outlandish stuff these days,* he thought. *Still it's their choice.*

It seemed chaotic to them as they went under the arched entrance to the paved courtyard, past a stone staircase on each side, one leading to the office of the Caravanserai and the other to a series of anti-rooms for the Merchants and their servants.

Groups of merchants and servants were unloading pack animals. Horses were nuzzling nose-bags of food, camels kneeling as their loads were taken off. A scurrying line of men carried sacks of goods to temporarily pile them against the courtyard walls between animal stalls and bays.

Shrill voices, echoing around the courtyard in several different languages, were arguing about prices or fees.

The smell of ordure permeated the air.

In the far corner of the courtyard, the travellers that Chaz and Esher had seen earlier were sorting themselves out. It seemed like organized chaos.

The head of the group could be heard shouting orders and directing his servants to do this or that.

'You won't believe this Esha but that guy over there is speaking in Italian.'

'Oh my God. It can't be, can it?'

'Give over, Esha, he's ancient. Fifty at least.'

'Yeah but are there any younger men there.'

'From what I can see from here, I think there are about nine or ten of them over there who might be fairly young looking for this time. Haven't you noticed? Look around you.'

Esha nodded and had a casual look round the courtyard.

Amongst the filth and dust that was being kicked up or being blown by the breeze that wafted in now and again, most of the men and she realized it was nearly all men, were bearded and wore a turban or hat of some kind. Their clothes, mostly ragged looking, apart from the merchants themselves, gave nothing away as to how old they might be.

'See what I mean.'

Esha nodded again.

'It's hopeless, isn't it? I mean, we don't even know what year it is, apart from looking around here, which looks as though it's a period of the past. Right.'

Chaz could only agree.

To keep out of the way they moved to one side past the stone steps and stood by large bundles stacked by the wall.

As they did so, a tall man came down the steps

carrying a scroll. A tuft of greying hair peeked out from the edge of his peak-less cap. A full beard was let down by a wispy moustache which gave him a whimsical expression.

The man stopped a couple of steps from the courtyard floor and called out, 'Signore Maffeo, Signore Maffeo.'

Among the group of travellers in the far corner of the courtyard, the leader turned round and waved.

'Yes, Jinhai Chen, what do you want?'

"I need an itinerary of your animals and men and of how long you intend to stay.'

'I shall be with you as soon as I have sorted these goods and animals.'

'Sooner rather than later please. We lock-down at sunset remember and I want to finish by then.'

Signore Maffeo acknowledged with a wave, as Jinhai Chen went back up the steps to his office.

6

'Jeez, did you hear that Esha.'

Chaz had grabbed her arm and rushed on in an excited voice.

'Maffeo, isn't that Marco Polo's uncle. My God, don't you see, we're actually in the time of Marco Polo. It's a chuffin' miracle, that's what it is, a chuffin' miracle.'

'Keep it down Chaz,' whispered Esha anxiously. 'That guard might hear you and get suspicious.'

She pulled at Chaz.

'Get down by these bundles for a minute, while I think.'

They crouched behind the pile of merchandise and looked to see if anyone was watching them.

Everyone was too occupied with their work to notice them and Esha relaxed somewhat.

'Chaz, Chaz,' whispered Esha. She had to nudge him for his attention.

He was preoccupied watching a horse relieve itself, fortunately over a slot in the courtyard floor, strategically placed there, for this very purpose.

'Oh, sorry, you don't see that every day where I live. What is it?'

'You must have heard him. That Maffeo, he said Jinhai Chen. My uncle's name, remember.'

The penny dropped. Chaz nearly jumped to his feet in excitement.

'That Jinhai Chen must be your ancestor, Esha.'

'Oooh, Chaz, does that mean that we will both disappear if I speak to him. You know, like in the movies.' Esha was half serious.

That wiped the grin off his face for a moment.

'Naw, I think that's just sci-fi stuff and nonsense. Anyway, that means Marco Polo must be around here doesn't it.'

They sat back against the wall in the shadow of a pile of stacked goods and watched for a while.

A sense of order could now be seen. More and more of the animals were led into their allotted stalls, as they were unloaded. The piles of goods dotted around the courtyard were being transferred to niches and chambers set aside for them.

Chaz gave Esha a nudge. 'Do you see what I can see?'

'Stop playing games, Chaz,' she whispered. 'At times you drive me mad with your innuendoes. Just tell me.'

He gave a shrug and half pointed across the courtyard.

'See that bloke, wearing a grey tunic over a white shirt and those sort of tight leggings. He's got one of those floppy hats on, you know, with a bit hanging over one ear.'

Esha looked over through a group of snuffling, grunting camels and saw him walking towards the gateway and nodded.

'Well, from what I saw of his face he can't be very old.'

A flicker of excitement went right through her body, as she leaned closer to Chaz.

'What do you mean?'

'He's got practically no beard to speak of or moustache. It's no more than a wispy goatee. I reckon he's about twenty years old.'

'Chaz, that must be Marco, must be,' she said,

crossing her fingers.

Nodding his head in agreement, Chaz pointed to the gateway and said quietly. 'We need to follow him but not too close. We stand out like sore thumbs with our modern clothes on.'

Esha looked around. Not far from the stone steps three, maybe four bundles of cloth were stacked, seemingly waiting for someone to take them away.

Checking that no one was looking their way, Esha eased her way over and saw what she had hoped for – a hole in the bundle.

A piece of white silk could be seen, so finger on lips to Chaz, Esha opened her daypack and found a small pair of scissors in a side pocket.

Then she beckoned to him.

'Help me pull this out,' she said, indicating the silk.

The sacking was tough but with a few snips with the scissors, Esha made the hole big enough for Chaz to pull a bolt of white silk out.

'What are you going to do with this?' asked a perplexed Chaz.

'Watch and learn,' smiled Esha as she unrolled a length of the white silk, measuring with her eyes.

Using her scissors, she cut a long piece off and held it to his body and nodded to herself.

'Just hold it out for me please Chaz,' she asked.

As he did so, Esha cut two slits in the sheet of silk. 'Now for the moment of truth,' she muttered.

'Put this on like a bath robe, Chaz,' she instructed, going back to her daypack while he did so.

With his hands through the slits, he now had a robe of sorts reaching nearly down to his boots, especially when fixed by the neck with the safety pin she had just got from her pack. Most of his modern clothes were now largely hidden.

It took her only a minute or two to make one for herself.

'I believe they used to call this sort of thing a surcote,' she said, as she fastened it by her neck with another safety pin.

7

By the time they had passed the guard at the Caravanserai entrance, Marco, for they were now convinced that was who he was, had disappeared.

'Sod it,' Chaz said with a groan of disappointment. 'Where the hell can he have got to?'

Esha looked left and right along the rough track made in the loose sand.

'There's only one place he could go,' she said with conviction.

'The moon lake.'

So, turning to the left, they made their way along the outside wall of the Caravanserai until they reached the end of it. The dune suddenly dipped and there, a couple of hundred metres in front was Marco striding down the slope towards the oasis.

The dune levelled out in a sort of platform, which was covered with a dense mix of saxaul and tamarix bushes, many three or four metres high. The unusual shaped lake was some twenty-five metres further down a gradual slope of the dune.

Esha and Chaz crouched down hoping not to be seen, as they watched Marco force his way through the thicket of bushes towards the lake. They were not sure what they were going to do when - if, they actually caught up with him.

Something happened by the lake.

A loud shout echoed round the dunes and Chaz stood up to get a better view.

'Can you see what's happening, Chaz?' Esha said, getting to her feet.

'It looks damn funny to me,' he replied. 'Marco's waving his arms about. Just a minute, now he's dancing.'

'What! He's dancing?' asked Esha incredulously.

'Sorry, that's wrong, not dancing. Jumping. Jumping like the devil.'

As they watched the cavorting figure of Marco by the edge of the lake, he suddenly screamed out, a cry of pure agony.

'My God, what the hell's happening? We have to go down and help him, Chaz,' cried Esha, who had already begun to run down towards the lake.

Chaz needed no more urging. The high-pitched cry in Italian, which went on and on without pause, drove him like a bat out of hell.

He overtook Esha and forced a way through the tangle of bushes until he reached the edge of the lake.

Marco lay writhing in obvious agony on the sand, his face covered with sand flies and both hands clutching his ankle in a vice like grip.

Next to him was a small snake, it's head crushed by the bloody rock, which lay by his feet.

Esha arrived, panting heavily, 'How is he?' She asked between breaths. Then she saw the snake. *A pit viper,* she thought.

Staying calm, her work as a veterinary assistant could prove the difference between life and death.

'Quick as you can Chaz, try and get his hands off his ankle and lean him against the trunk of that big bush while I get that box of antitoxin inhibitors that Uncle Jinhai gave me from my pack. My God, he must have second sight or something.'

As fast as she could, Esha threw off her makeshift robe and pulled the pack off her shoulders

Chaz had bent down and tried to waft away the swarm of sand flies that had settled on Marco's face, unable to avoid watching Marco twitching in agony as the venom began to take hold.

He scratched at his own face as he began to get bitten and then managed to loosen Marco's grip on his ankle. As gently as he could, he then put his hands under his arms and lifted him sideways to the bush that Esha had indicated.

Marco groaned and began to breathe rapidly.

'Scuse me,' Esha said, as she pushed past him.

'We haven't much time. Pull up his leggings, carefully now. We mustn't move him too much.'

As soon as the ankle was free, Esha picked out one of her uncle's purple patches of antitoxin inhibitors. Removing the purple covering she placed the patch gently over the nasty snake-bite puncture wound.

Esha looked over at Chaz.

'Uncle Jinhai told me this was very special and effective if put on as soon as possible after the bite. The patch will, he told me, dissolve by itself. That it was part of the treatment. It mustn't be touched before then, so I'd better cover it with something to hide what I've done.'

Esha delved into her pack again and pulled out a linen shirt and with a shrug, cut a strip from it.

Having tied the bandage, *she couldn't leave a twenty-first century safety pin;* She looked at Chaz and said, 'Now I will have to report this to the Caravanserai. They will have to look after Marco from now on.'

Chaz started to protest.

'Only I can speak old Mandarin. I have to go. You look after Marco, okay.'

That had to make sense to him, so he nodded in

agreement as Esha put her pack and then her white silk surcote on and ran up the sand dune towards the Caravanserai as fast as she could.

8

At first, the Caravanserai manager, Jinhai Chen ignored her plea to bring Marco up from the lake.

He had just come down the stone steps by the gateway and was getting annoyed by Esha's persistent requests for help. *Women should not be here,* he thought, *they get in the way of the efficient running of a Caravanserai.*

She had a funny way of speaking as well, a dialect he found difficult to understand. Then he recognized the word Maffeo.

Jinhai Chen paused. Signore Maffeo was an important traveller. He carried the seal of the Great Kublai Khan. Thinking he had better check this out, Chen sent a message requesting the presence of Signore Maffeo.

He came at once.

When Esha explained the urgency of Marco's injury to Signore Maffeo, all hell broke loose.

Two guards were summoned and ordered to select a camel chair at once and to carry it down to the lake.

Signore Maffeo in his anxiety, grabbed Caravanserai Chen by the arm and gave orders for him to be taken to Marco at once.

A flustered Chen looked at Esha and said, 'You will have to show us where to go.'

A much relieved Esha just nodded and rushed to the gateway, the others following as best they could.

Chaz was getting anxious. Esha seemed to have been gone for ages. He had wet his handkerchief in the lake and dabbed Marco's forehead with water.

Worryingly, Marco did not stir. He just lay there propped up by the gnarled trunk of the bush, sweat beading his face.

A rustling sound and voices broke the silence. Chaz stood just as Esha and the elderly man known as Maffeo burst into view, followed by Chen and the two guards who had trouble pulling the camel chair through the branches of the bushes.

'Marco, Marco.' Uncle Maffeo fell to his knees and grabbed hold of Marco's hand.

'Marco,' he called again.

Esha suddenly called Chen to her and whispered something to him.

Chen shook his head but Esha insisted and pointed to the dead snake.

This time he nodded and said, 'Signore Maffeo we must take Marco to the Caravanserai at once if you want to save his life.'

Marco's uncle saw the sense in that and ordered the two guards to put Marco in the camel chair that they had carried down.

The cane chair, one of a pair that are usually fixed on the camel back to back, was big enough for Marco to be strapped in and it also incorporated a foot-rest, so that his legs would be securely tied as well.

Esha standing next to Chaz, was relieved to see that. She was aware that snake-bite victims were not to be moved unless absolutely necessary.

The two guards went to pick up Marco who had still not uttered a sound, when one stopped and handed a short sword to Chen and indicated that he go first and chop a way through the thicket of bushes.

Chen nodded and immediately began to hack a way through, wide enough for the guards carrying Marco to safely follow when they were ready.

Uncle Maffeo went next, muttering to himself in Italian some sort of prayer.

Progress was slow up the dune but eventually they reached the Caravanserai without any accidents and as Esha and Chas watched, Marco was taken inside.

Before Chaz could say anything, Esha turned and pointed to the sun. It was sinking behind the huge dune on the far side of the Crescent Moon Lake.

'It can't be that late,' cried Chaz in amazement. 'We haven't been here that long surely?'

'I'm not going to argue but remember what the old man Sulu, said,' answered Esha.

'Yeah and now we're up shit creek without a chuffin' paddle. What the hell do we do now?'

'Come on Chaz; think for God's sake. How did we get here?'

'Of course. The portal. We've got to get to the portal.'

Esha smiled to herself. 'I knew you'd get there eventually Chaz.'

'Now who's being funny. Come on we don't have much time. That's assuming the damn thing is still there and it still chuffin' works.'

'Don't say that, Chaz.' For the first time Esha felt uneasy and anxious.

Going down the sand dune made it easier and quicker than the first time they had come this way. The stone lined sewer trench was easy to follow.

The stench coming from it didn't smell any better the second time round either.

As they walked down, Esha remembered the document written by this historical Jinhai Chen.

'I say Chaz, that old document that my Uncle

showed us.'

Yeah, what of it?'

'Well, in the excitement of knowing who he might be, I sort of glossed over some of the things he had written.'

'Such as,' prompted Chaz.

'We know from history, that Marco stayed in Dunhuang for about a year after getting over an illness. Well, this Jinhai Chen wrote that two passing Shamans helped heal a lethal foot injury of Marco Polo and that one had red hair and who never spoke and the other was a woman with a hunch-back.'

'So,'

'Look at us Chaz what do you see.'

'Err, two dirty faces,'

'Chaz, for God's sake be serious for once.'

'Okay, okay,' he grinned and said, 'we both look like a pair of monks lost in the wilderness with these white silk robes on.'

Then the penny dropped. 'Jeez, you've a bump on your back. The daypack. Of course, he never saw you without these robes on did he?' Chaz said, patting her on the back.

'Chuffin' hell, what a carry on.'

'Yes, because of your size, yours didn't stick out as much as mine. '

'So you're the mystery female Shaman.'

'I suppose I am,' Esha said, bowing to her red-headed assistant before reflecting; 'That's if we ever get back.'

That shut Chaz up for a while until they reached the stinking pond.

'It must be round here somewhere,' Esha said apprehensively, looking at every bush in sight.

The sun had reached the top of the dune on the other side of the hollow they were in, making long shadows of the saxaul bushes.

Chaz felt the tightening of his stomach and taking a deep breath, turned round, fingers crossed in the age-old belief of hope in adversity.

There, in the shadows a flicker of light – a violet light.'

'Hallelujah,' cried Chaz. 'There is a God after all. Look Esha, over there. It's the portal. Come on let's get the hell out of here. Now.'

The gnarled saxaul branches hid most of the portal but the flickering light was as good as a flaming beacon as far as Chaz was concerned as they went behind the bush.

Holding Esha by the arm, he jumped first over the edge of the portal pulling her through as he did so.

And landed on the carpet inside the tent.

The old man was just picking up the last of the broken tea bowls and he straightened up, smiling.

He bowed towards them, unfazed by the fact that they were still wearing the makeshift white silk robes.

'I Sulu, welcome you back to my humble abode. I trust you had an eventful journey. I see from the look on your faces you did. It was well that that you took my advice and left before sunset. You were very wise to do so.'

The old man called Sulu put the broken pieces of porcelain on the table and said, 'I too have a journey to make and must say goodbye to you.'

He held up a hand - palm outwards - fingers together with the thumb tight to the fingers. Then he opened the middle two fingers into the peace sign and said in a voice that could hardly be heard.

'May your ancestors rest in peace.'

Then he walked to the portal and jumped through to another place and another time.

It was as though someone had turned a switch. The tent began to shake and shudder and Chaz suddenly had a funny feeling.

'For God's sake move,' he shouted to Esha.

As if coming out of a dream, Esha suddenly screamed as she saw the top of the tent suddenly collapse and begin to fall down towards them.

There was nothing to do but run and she ran to the entrance.

Chaz needed no more urging either and he ran after her and they both stood by the roadside and gaped in disbelief as the whole shabby mass of the tent fell into a whirlpool of dust and sand, which then became a flickering discharge of electrical energy that for a moment, dazzled them in its intensity before fading away.

A clear patch of sand was all that remained when they regained their vision.

'What the hell was all that about,' Chaz said, scratching his head.

I've not the faintest idea Chaz but I know what I fancy now. A few glasses of apricot-peel water mixed with vodka or maybe that new Japanese whisky.

'Now that is what I call a good idea,' agreed Chaz as they began to walk on past a newspaper display board.

One caption caught his eye. It was a picture of the Crescent Moon Lake with a cloud of dark smoke drifting over it.

'I say Esha, what's that about?'

'Just a minute while I see,' she said.

'Oh, it says that a gaz cylinder explosion caused little damage. A small fire was quickly extinguished.'

'So that was what scared us to death. Hey, without that we might never have met up with Marco. What a chuffin' coincidence.'

'Come on Chaz, I'm dying for that drink.'

'My God, I don't believe it,' he suddenly cried out as he jumped to get out of the way of someone who was in a hurry.

'That cretin has just gobbed on my boot.'

The Author

Watercolour painting

Rita Clements Lee
ritaclementslee-artist.co.uk

Also by Rita Clements Lee

Muses in Watercolour

The Kiss of the Sun

Lost in France

eBook or Paperback)

***

Further Reading

Extract from Trimefirst.
Brian Leon lee

Taking his ion gun from his hip holster, Fancy left the room and went down to the alleyway. He looked carefully along the narrow, dingy passage. Deciding it was safe enough to go, he crept along keeping to one side of the alley and as low as possible. It was the strange sort of hissing noise that caused him to look up. He froze in shock. There, about three metres above him was a hovering alien. It was hanging there, sitting in that peculiar flying thing. Two pairs of large compound eyes were staring right at him. Then the antennae began to bend down and point towards him................

Extract from Domain of the Netherworld.
Brian Leon

.... Bryden stood up and running towards the monster, threw his spear. It hurtled through the air and pierced the man-vamp's left wing and then his lower back. A shriek of agony split the air as the creature tried to take flight. The spear shaft had pinned the left wing to the man-vamps body so it couldn't fly.

It turned round, one wing flapping fruitlessly. Then, snarling and chittering, it tottered unsteadily on taloned feet towards him, unused to walking on them. Its canines clashed with desire to get hold of his throat as it drooled and slobbered on its mission to kill..................

Printed in Great Britain
by Amazon

27196366R00030